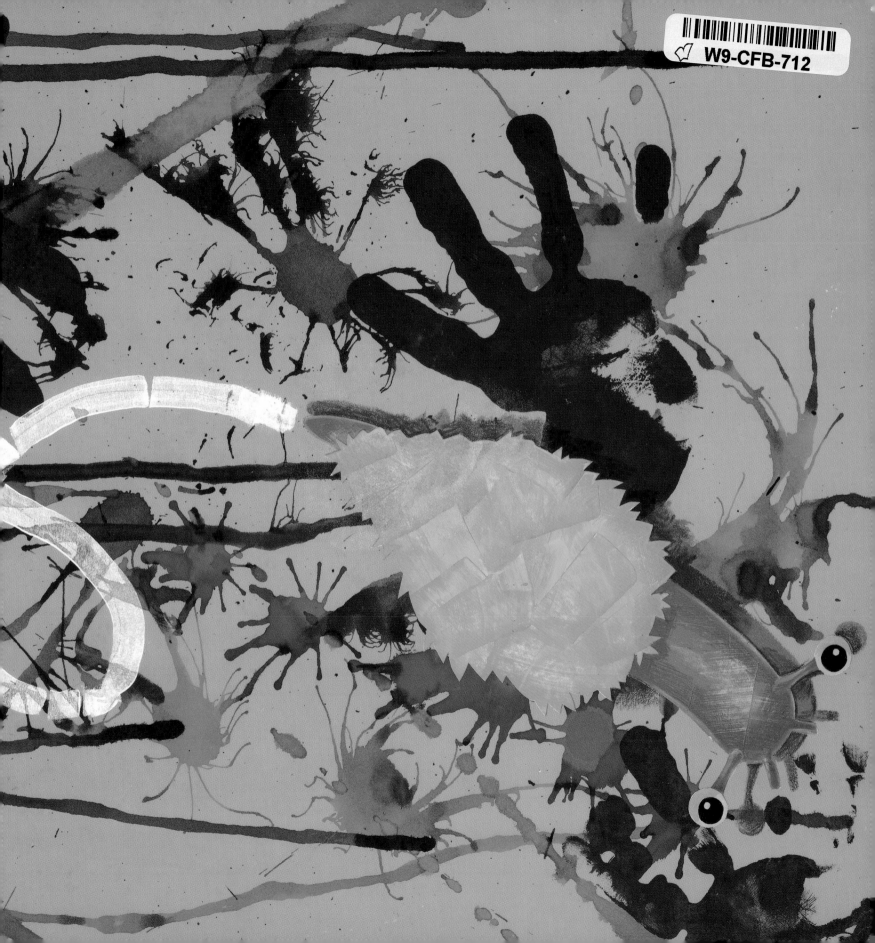

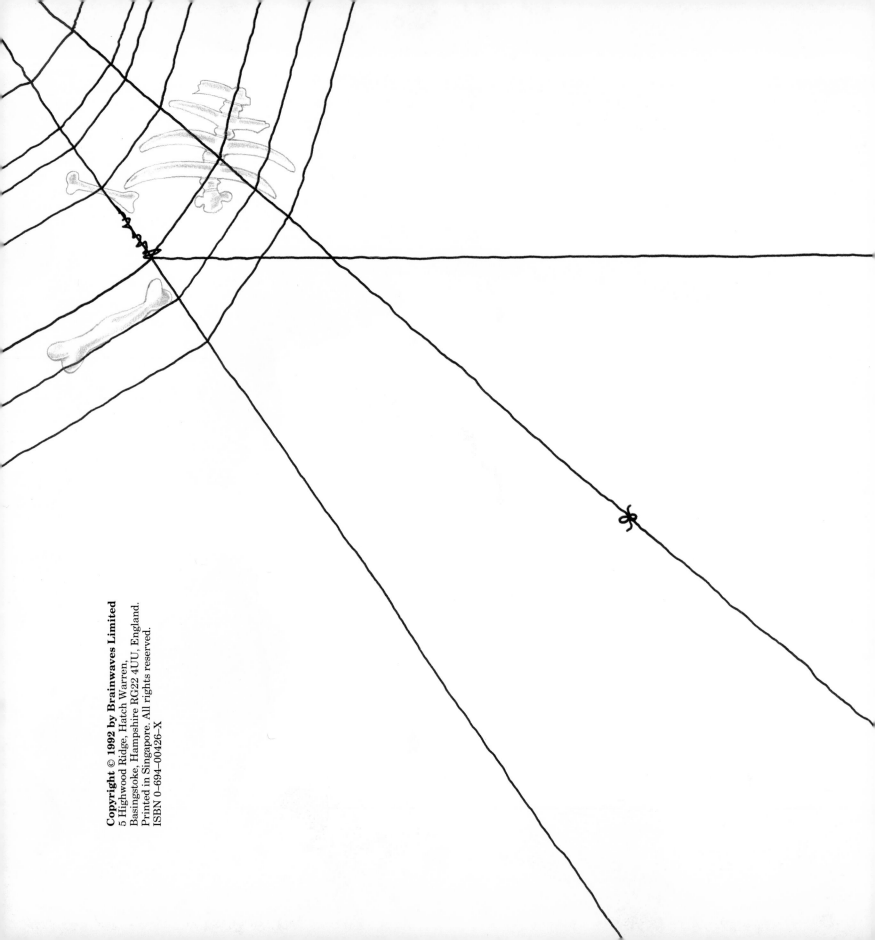

MY NEW NEIGHBORS

Written by Keith Faulkner

Illustrated by Jonathan Lambert

HarperFestival

A Division of HarperCollins*Publishers*

We've moved to a new neighborhood.
Mom says the change will do us good.

I have no friends now, living near.
I hope I make some new friends here.

Behind our home a strange house stands,
Like a castle in a foreign land.

I wonder who lives on the hill;
To look at it gives me a chill.

It wasn't very long at all
Till my new neighbors came to call.

They must have come to our front door
To leave the note there on the floor.

I saw the hand that brought the mail.
I caught a glimpse of greenish scale.

Perhaps that hand was just a joke.
If not, our neighbors are strange folk.

I heard footsteps that shook the floor
And then a loud knock at the door.

He was the biggest thing I'd seen.
His face was grinning, huge, and green.

He said, "I hope that soon, one day,
You'll ask me over here to play."

A ghoulish gift for girls and boys;
It's one of my most favorite toys.

When the next neighbor came to call,
There really was no sound at all.

No sound of steps, I wonder why.
You'd think she'd flown down from the sky.

"This gift, my dear, I've brought for you
Is something all kids like to do."

"If you have problems, don't despair;
I'm quite an expert . . . in the air."

I must admit I got a shock
When the next neighbor came to knock.

Outside the door I heard a growl
And then a loud bloodcurdling howl.

There was a small boy standing there,
With pointed ears and wild red hair.

"This gift's for you," he said with glee.
"I take mine in the tub with me."

Later that night, I thought I heard
The sound of flapping, like a bird.

I went downstairs — what a surprise —
A tall, dark man with glowing eyes.

"Ah! You're awake; I saw a light."
He said, "You see, I work at night."

The gift he gave looked like a bat.
He said, "You'll have some fun with that."

I'd been asleep for quite some time,
But woke to hear the old clock chime.

And in my bedroom floating near,
I saw a ghostly girl appear.

She gave a smile so full of charm.
Her head was tucked beneath her arm.

"This gift's for you," I heard her call
As she departed through the wall.

I'm sure that it is plain to see
No one's got neighbors quite like me.

It's true they're weird and stay up late,
But my new neighbors are really great.

There's nowhere I would rather be,
Than living near this family.

And I can guess — I'm sure it's true —
You wish that you could live here too!